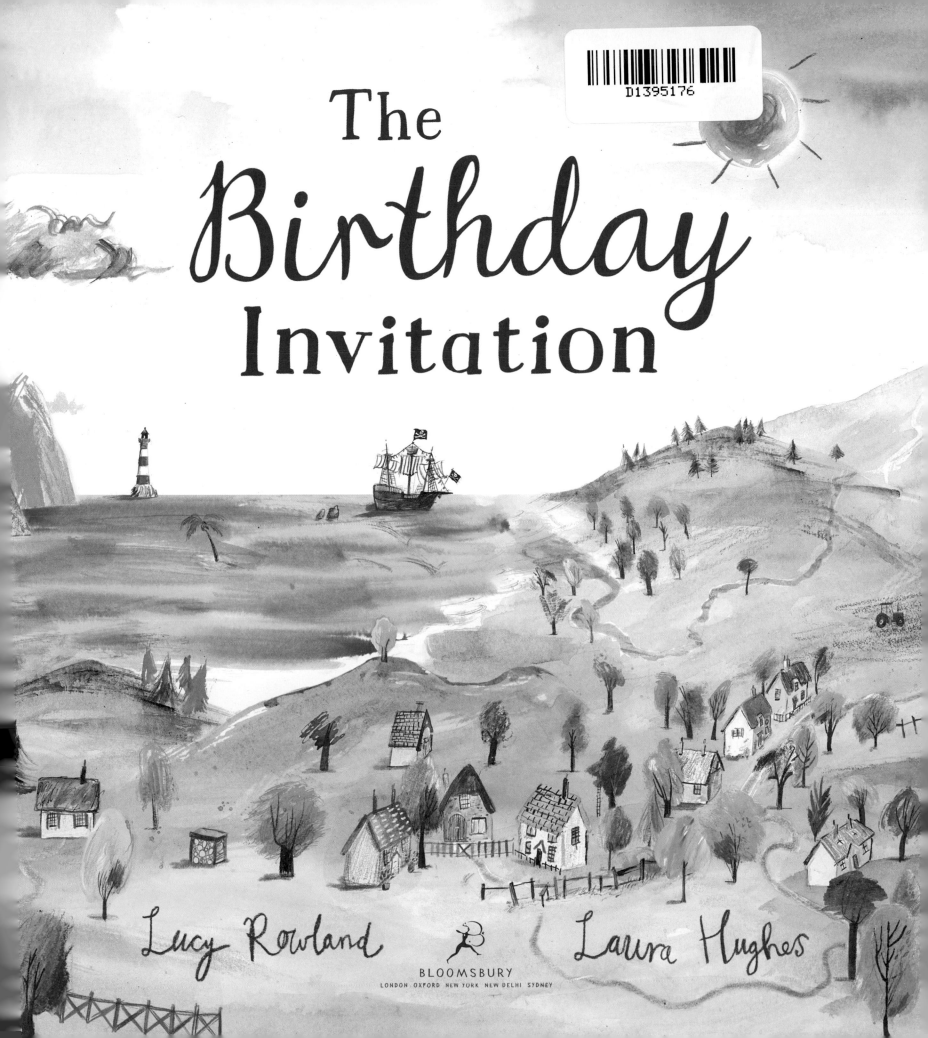

The Birthday Invitation

Lucy Rowland

BLOOMSBURY
LONDON OXFORD NEW YORK NEW DELHI SYDNEY

Laura Hughes

Ella woke one morning feeling ever so excited!
Tomorrow was her party,
all her friends would be invited!

She wrote her invitations . . .

then she set off eagerly,
To ask her friends to join her
for a special birthday tea.

But as she hurried through the wood,
   one note fell to the ground.
It lay among some toadstools,
   simply waiting to be found.

Quite soon a wizard came along,
collecting herbs and flowers,
And cried, "Oh look! Some toadstools.
Why, they're full of magic powers!

What's this? *An invitation?*
Ah, to Ella's birthday tea."

He popped it in a bottle,
laughing,
"Lucky,

lucky

ME!"

Much later, near the river,
as the wizard cast a spell,
He waved his arms above his head
– and out the bottle fell!

It splashed into the water
and then floated out to sea . . .

Where pirates caught it in their net
while fishing for their tea.

"A message in a bottle!"
called the captain to
his crew . . .

But then his parrot snatched the note

and

whooooosh

away she flew!

She landed at the castle
where a royal servant caught her,
And gave the invitation to
the King's excited daughter.

"How wonderful!"
the Princess cried,
but as she clapped her hands . . .

The invitation blew away
towards enchanted lands.

A knight spotted the letter and he read it to his horse –
"Please come along to Ella's tea?"
    "Why, yes!" he grinned. "Of course!"

He carried on his hunting and he shot an arrow high,

But now the invitation was careering through the sky!

A pilot caught the letter
as it soared up past her plane.
She read the invitation . . .

then the note
flew off again.
She watched it
zooming

down,

down,

down . . .

. . . faster than a rocket!

And Ella didn't see it when
it landed in her pocket!

At last she
reached her friend's house
with the *final* invitation . . .

She asked him, "Can *you* join me
for my **birthday celebration?**"

They were both excited and they giggled with delight,
Then talked about the party games they'd play tomorrow night.

The next day Ella rushed around – "There's SO much to get ready!"
"I can't wait for my party!" Ella whispered to her teddy.

She hung up decorations –
streamers, flags and
huge balloons!

Then waited at the table.
All her friends would be here soon!

But when she heard the
KNOCK KNOCK KNOCK,
it sounded far too loud,

And opening the door she saw . . .

...a VERY lively crowd!

They shouted, "Happy Birthday! Look, we've brought you round a cake!"

But Ella, though delighted, said, "I think there's some mistake . . ."

So after lots of giggling they started from the start,
And each explained to Ella how they'd played their special part.

The wizard found it first.
The parrot took it from the pirate.

The princess next and then the knight –
and don't forget the pilot.

Ella sighed, "I can't believe
I dropped an invitation!"
And then *she* started laughing, too . . .

"But what a

celebration!"